Bullfrog at Magnolia Circle

SMITHSONIAN INSTITUTION

SMITHSONIAN'S BACKYARD

Illustrations copyright © 2002 Kristin Kest.
Book copyright © 2012 Palm Publishing, Norwalk, Connecticut, USA
and the Smithsonian Institution, Washington DC 20560.

Published by Soundprints, an imprint of Palm Publishing, Norwalk, Connecticut.
www.palmkids.com

Series design, book layout: Shields & Partners
Editors: Laura Gates Galvin & Judy Gitenstein

First Edition 2002
10 9 8 7 6 5 4 3
Printed in the USA

Acknowledgments:
  Our very special thanks to Dr. George Zug of the Department of Systematic Biology at the Smithsonian Institution's
National Museum of Natural History for his biological review, and our very special thanks to Kristin Kest for her
amazing work under pressure.
  Soundprints would also like to thank Ellen Nanney and Robyn Bissette at the Smithsonian Institution's Office
of Product Development and Licensing for their help in the creation of this book.

Library of Congress Cataloging-in-Publication Data

Dennard, Deborah.
        Bullfrog at Magnolia Circle / by Deborah Dennard ; illustrated by Kristin Kest.
              p.   cm.
        Summary: A young male bullfrog avoids a hungry heron and searches for a calling site in his bayou home.
        ISBN 1-931465-04-5 — ISBN 1-931465-05-3 (micro hardcover)
    1. Bullfrog—Juvenile fiction. [1. Bullfrog—Fiction. 2. Frogs—Fiction.] I. Kest, Kristin, ill. II. Title.

PZ10.3.D386 Bu 2002
[E]—dc21

                                                                                        2001049691

Bullfrog at Magnolia Circle

by Deborah Dennard
Illustrated Kristin Kest

Soundprints™

4

Lightning zigzags through the early evening sky over the bayou waters that slowly wind their way behind the white wooden house on Magnolia Circle. Thunder rumbles in the distance. The croaking of bullfrogs, and the peeps and sounds of other frogs, fill the air.

5

In midwinter, Bullfrog emerged from his muddy winter retreat and silently waited for the warmth and rains of spring. Now in April, his throat yellow and bulging, he sings a sound like *"brrwoom."*

After a summer and a fall as a tadpole and over a year as a youngster, Bullfrog is now fully grown. Using his long webbed back feet, he swims through the duckweed to the edge of the bayou.

As Bullfrog pulls his long body up the bank of the bayou, a crayfish emerges from a chimney made of mud. In less than half a second, Bullfrog springs forward. His long, sticky tongue shoots out and grabs the crayfish.

The crayfish struggles, but Bullfrog uses his front legs to stuff the crustacean into his mouth. As he swallows, his large bulging eyeballs sink into his head to push the crayfish farther down his throat.

Rain cascades from the sky, soaking the earth. In the distance, by the large screened porch, huge oak trees covered by Spanish moss sway in the warm, heavy air. Bullfrog hops past the dock. He moves slowly, closing his eyes with each hop as the rain drips onto his smooth, green skin.

A bolt of lightning illuminates the sky. A few seconds later, a loud crash of thunder explodes. The warm, wet evening is perfect for Bullfrog to explore the bayou. Tonight he will begin his search for a calling site, and then he can start singing to attract his first mate.

A sphinx moth flutters past Bullfrog and lands on a blade of a wild weed near the water. Bullfrog sees the moth with his big, round eyes. In an instant, his long, sticky tongue brings the moth to his mouth and it becomes part of his evening meal.

As Bullfrog eats the moth, he does not notice the silent landing of a black-crowned heron. But the heron notices Bullfrog. A nice, fat, juicy bullfrog would satisfy a hungry heron.

Ever so slowly, the heron stalks its prey. His neck is pulled back and he is ready to make a swift, killing stab. The heron moves slowly closer to unsuspecting Bullfrog.

21

Suddenly, a loud crash by the garage of the house echoes in the night. A fat raccoon scurries away from the trash can lid she just knocked over. The loud noise startles both Bullfrog and the heron. Squawking a loud complaint, the heron takes to the air, leaving Bullfrog behind, unharmed.

The bullfrog, startled by the departing heron, leaps into the water, but soon returns to the shore. He hears the clicking sounds of southern cricket frogs in the grass. One of the little frogs jumps. It lands just in front of Bullfrog. In less than a second, it is in Bullfrog's mouth.

From the booming croaks all around, Bullfrog knows other male bullfrogs are nearby. While calling for his mate, Bullfrog might have to wrestle with one of these males, or he might simply do battle with his deep bass voice, calling and calling.

Bullfrog hops back to the water and dives in, landing with a splash. A special layer of skin protects Bullfrog's open eyes so he can see underwater. He swims farther out into the bayou, through a cluster of water lilies. At the edge of the water lilies, he stops.

He has been searching for a special place. This could be it. In this special place he will attract a female bullfrog by calling to her in his deep voice. She will come and deposit her eggs.

He rises to the surface, spreads his legs out and floats effortlessly. His throat bulges. He croaks again and again, *"brrwoom, brrwoom."*

The voices of other males join in and a bass chorus fills the air. Soon, with luck, a female will hear Bullfrog and come to him. For now he will stay close by this spot and call and wait in the bayou waters behind the white, wooden house on Magnolia Circle.

Fun Facts About the Bullfrog

Bullfrogs begin life as one of approximately 10,000 to 20,000 tiny eggs laid in a thin jelly-like film amongst plants floating on the surface of a body of slow-moving water. About four to eight days later, tiny tadpoles emerge from the eggs. Bullfrogs may spend one to three years as tadpoles, depending on where they live. It may take another three years for the frogs to become adults and to mate.

These amphibians are the largest frogs in North America. They may grow 5 to 6 inches long and may measure 12 inches with legs outstretched. Male bullfrogs have larger tympana, or external ears than do female bullfrogs. Bullfrogs have white to yellowish throats and underbellies, and a smooth-skinned back in shades of green.

Male bullfrogs communicate by croaking—forcing air back and forth across their vocal folds. Some people describe the sound as *"brrwoom."*

Their calls are used to proclaim territory and attract females.

Bullfrogs are excellent hunters and eat just about anything they can cram into their mouths. They sit and wait for a prey animal to come close enough, then pounce and catch their meal with their long, quick, sticky tongues, all in about one-half of a second. Bullfrogs help to control insects that are pests. They also eat lizards, snails, snakes, fish, mice and even other frogs.

Because they are highly prized by people for the meat in their long legs, they have been moved to many places outside of their natural homes. The bullfrog population in places such as California and Taiwan has become so great, that bullfrogs have become pests themselves, leaving little food or space for other native frogs.

Glossary

amphibian: An animal with a backbone, moist skin and usually two life stages

bayou: A marshy course of water leading to a lake or river

crustacean: An animal without a backbone, often living inside a shell

tadpole: An immature amphibian in a stage after egg but before adult. Tadpoles live and breathe underwater. Adult amphibians may live in or near water but breathe air.

tympanum: An external eardrum. The large circles on the side of a frog's head just behind the eyes are the tympanum.

Points of Interest in this Book

pp. 4-5: bayou
pp. 8-9: crayfish and its burrow (bottom right)
pp. 10-11: bullfrog's eyes sinking into his head when he swallows
pp. 14-15: oak tree; Spanish moss
pp. 16-17: sphinx moth (tobacco hornworm); bullfrog's projectile tongue

pp. 18-19: black-crowned heron
pp. 22-23: raccoon
pp. 24-25: southern cricket frog
pp. 26-27: calling male bullfrogs with vocal sacs
pp. 30-31: water lily (far left)